CECIL COUNTY
W9-DFO-718

# HALLOWEEN NIGHT

Elizabeth Hatch

ILLUSTRATED BY

Jimmy Pickering

A Doubleday Book for Young Readers

A Doubleday Book for Young Readers

Published by
Random House Children's Books
a division of
Random House, Inc.
New York

Doubleday and the anchor with dolphin colophon are registered trademarks of Random House, Inc.

Text copyright © 2005 by Elizabeth Hatch
Illustrations copyright © 2005 by Jimmy Pickering

All rights reserved. No part of this book may be reproduced or transmitted in any form or by any means, electronic or mechanical, including photocopying, recording, or by any information storage and retrieval system, without the written permission of the publisher, except where permitted by law.

Visit us on the Web! www.randomhouse.com/kids
Educators and librarians, for a variety of teaching tools, visit us at www.randomhouse.com/teachers

Library of Congress Cataloging-in-Publication Data is available upon request.

ISBN: 0-385-74622-9 (trade)
0-385-90887-3 (lib. bdg.)

The text of this book is set in 33-point Tremble.
Book design by Trish Parcell Watts
MANUFACTURED IN MALAYSIA
August 2005
10 9 8 7 6 5 4 3 2

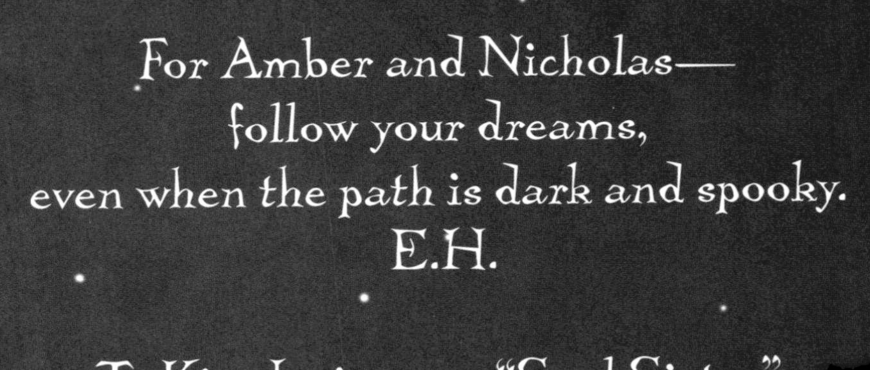

For Amber and Nicholas—
follow your dreams,
even when the path is dark and spooky.
E.H.

To Kim Irvine: my "Soul Sister"
and the true Diva of color
J.P.

It's Halloween night!

This is a jack-o'-lantern.

This is the mouse

who hides inside the jack-o'-lantern.

This is the bat
who dips and dives up in the sky

above the mouse
hiding inside the jack-o'-lantern.

This is the owl

who hoots at the bat

who dips and dives up in the sky
above the mouse

hiding inside the jack-o'-lantern.

This is the cat, all inky black,

who stalks the owl

who hoots at the bat

who dips and dives up in the sky

above the mouse

hiding inside the jack-o'-lantern.

This is the child, draped in white,

who loves the cat, all inky black,

who stalks the owl

who hoots at the bat
who dips and dives up in the sky
above the mouse

hiding inside the jack-o'-lantern.

This is the dog, begging for treats,

who trips the child,

who spills the treats

and startles the cat,

who spooks the owl,

who frightens the bat,

who swoops away up, up across the sky.

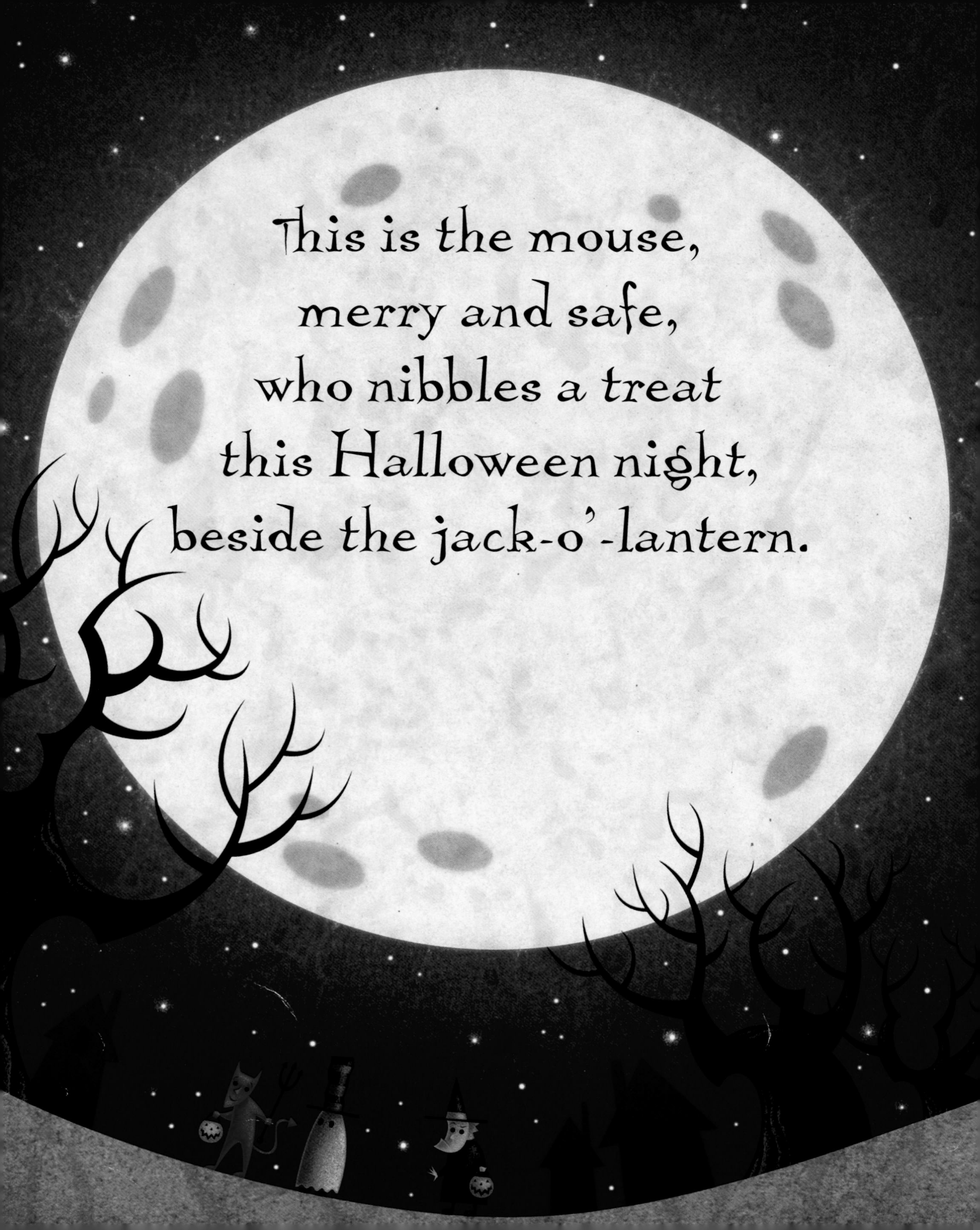

This is the mouse,
merry and safe,
who nibbles a treat
this Halloween night,
beside the jack-o'-lantern.

RIS
E Fic HAT
Hatch, Elizabeth
Halloween night.